An Elusive Repose

SATABDI MOHANTY

An Imprint of

MAPLE PRESS PRIVATE LIMITED
office: A 63, Sector 58, Noida 201 301, U.P., India
phone: +91 120 455 3581, 455 3583
email: info@maplepress.co.in
website: www.maplepress.co.in

An Elusive Repose *by* Satabdi Mohanty

Copyright © Satabdi Mohanty 2020

ISBN: 978-93-90292-00-4

10 9 8 7 6 5 4 3 2 1

Cover Design @ Umesh Semwal

Image Courtesy Shutterstock

Dedicated to

To my parents, Gita Rani Mohanty and
Prasanna Kumar Mohanty, for letting me dream...

Contents

Acknowledgement

This book is the result of limitless imagination and deep-rooted compassion, and both these elements are gifted by my parents. I would like to thank God for blessing me with opportunities in life, my parents for always letting me fly, and giving me the space to commit mistakes and learn from them, my brothers and sisters who give me tremendous courage, my husband, Ajay for always believing in me, other family members, my teachers, my best mates Shipra and Mridula, who are the first ones to listen to all my poems and all my dear friends for supporting me throughout this journey.

David…

Blind & weedy; the clock is ticking
Old & peaky; the hope is waning
No friends or family; Just David keeps barking
No calls or visits; Just David keeps comforting

Ambitious & greedy; my son is flying
Selfish & ungrateful; my son is growing
Tired & Forlorn; my body is tearing
Memories of John is slowly fading

Piteous & weary; my grave is waiting
With my tears, David keeps mourning
My melancholic opera runs all night
Solitary audience David stands by my side

Knock at door; David keeps fearing
Tap at floor; David keeps barking
Death at portal; David keeps scowling
David is loyal; David keeps loving

Son forgets; David remembers
Man deceives; David protects
He lives for me; I live for him
He sees for me; I see the world through him

Wild & Dark; blackest of nights
Anxious & Frozen; David kept crying
Death was steps away; tearful were his eyes
David was daunted; so was I

Click Clack; footsteps were approaching
Abandoned & helpless, who was coming!
Louder got the tapping; David kept growling
Guest is my death; I was surmising

No money or gems I was possessing
Breaking into an old home; what was he stealing!
Scared & Shaky; louder got my yelling
David ran towards him, howling & howling

Chained by blindness; I cursed the darkness
Run David! Run! I mourned in blackness
Shrouded with lust; He ravaged my life
He came for David, not for my life

Strangled my David, light of my life
Ravished my David; stick of the blind
Visitor was the death; David died
Till last breath, he defended me

Blind & weedy; the clock is broken
Old & peaky; the hope is shaken
No friends or family; David stopped barking
No calls or visits; David died comforting.

Forever…

Kisses my forehead; wipes my tears
Warmth of his breath; I feel in my ears
Hugs me tight; doffs all my fears
Love in his eyes has intensified in years

Every passing second, he inspires
Love is not easy; he conspires
Killed his dreams; he owned mine
I am his life; he wants me to shine

"Beautiful you are since break of dawn
Soul of yours is pure as swans'
Heart thrills with your radiant smile"
His favorite words- he forever recites

Lifts my heart; takes me to unknown time
Flaunts a world that is different from mine
Flaws and Stains are not undermined
Weakness and Feebleness are no more crime

"Forget the incident; forget that while
Erase that moment; that killed your smile
Begged for your breath; prayed for your life
God listened" he gratifies

Closes my eyes; forges my fantasies
"Body is frilly costume; not worthwhile
Fate is not the king, commander of life
Strength is within" I realize

Past is gone; he forbids to mourn
No arms no legs; he claims "my voice is weapon"
Mind is poetic; his hands will blossom
Time was harsh; his love is salvation

Night and day; he stays here
Night and day; he strolls near
Kisses on forehead; wipes my tears
Hugs me tight; doffs all my fears.

My Age of Ignorance

Years ago when I was young
Pen became ally, thoughts weapon
Committed was I to write songs or poems
I started the journey with utter devotion
Hopping on the clouds of my imagination
I completed thousands of words of my vision
Pen was my only mate, books far beyond my apprehension
Hours and hours, I scribbled my reflection
Beautifully written, I suppose yet never my final conclusion

One day, I held a book that became mine
Spent hours, yet hundreds of pages undetermined
Scant dedication, yet travelled with Pips' affluent time
"Great Expectation" finished Pips' journey with tears in my eyes
Power of book, I soon realized, Writer was I candid yet naive
Thoughts were my gift and words my emotion
Books revised my armor, made my pen mightier
Books adorned my talent and now I smile back at My Age of
Ignorance...

Special Soul

Drowned in innocence, blessed with ignorance
Her feet are always in sky
Jolted by curiosity, zestful by imagination
Her spirits are always high

Talking to the walls, dancing with the wind
She spends her lone time
Drawing in the cloud, singing to nature
She reminds me of my childhood time

Melodious is the earth, Joyful is the sun
She cherishes their amity all the time
Beautiful are the stars, heartful is the moon
She is the reflection of mine

I was the same, enjoyed the company of the sea
Clock ticked, and I use to still see
Unusual was I, never accepted by thee
Rare is she, so will be protected by me

Special is she, the world denies to accept
Pure is she, the world doesn't respect
Labeling her sick, the world enjoys
Declaring her weak, the world teases

Laughing at her, cruel folks pass by
Undermining her, her friends walk by
At 8, she is fragile to stand by
At 30, I will prepare her to fight by.

Live Life Again

Stronger than ever, fearless than ever
I shall stand up again.
Larger than ever, happier than ever
I shall live my life again.

Soon the gloomy days will evanesce and my life shall smile back at
me again.
Soon the pain will vanish away and love will find its way again.

Now every dawn will bring back my lost courage and faith.
Now every day my shadow will sing my saga of achievements.
Now nothing can come in my way as I am ready to fight again.

I'll never sacrifice my peace and I'll never kill my passion again.
I have already spent ages in the room of darkness, and now when I
have got the key to brightness
I can't afford to lose it again.
I might fall again but I promise to myself
I will never stop loving myself again.

Urge…

In the soundless night, I lay lonely by his side
In the silvery night, I stare blankly at the moonlight
In the callous bed, he crawls deep into me
In the closed chambers, he religiously mangles me

Shedding the bitter tears, I smile to myself
Hovering in the gnawing agony, I relax myself
Things I do for love, now have gone far away
Things I do for her, now have gone miles away

In the warm days, my eyes hunt for her
In the lazy springs, my arms desire her
Every battle in night, I survive for her
Every scar in my life, I hide for her

Kissing her supple lips, is always in my mind
Holding her tight, is my sole right
Touching her soft heart, damps me
Playing with her curls, entices me

Love for her, defines me
Charm of her, beguiles me
Nobody knows what she is to me
She is mine and always be mine

I am her sea and she will immerse in me
I am her destiny and she will outshine with me
People who try to take her from me
Will meet the hell untimely

Unknown of the feelings, she lets him inside
Ignorant of the meaning, she stays quiet
She worships him, and he mishandles me
He touches her, and the spite burns me alive

Unaware of love, she twiddles her thumb for him
Innocence of her, blinded her to see the real him
His love is no true, wrapped up with lust
My love is all pure, ornamented with trust

Though her heart is filled with hatred for me
Though she secretly wishes death for me
Though she thinks I am the hindrance for their love to win
She doesn't know what she is to me

Breaking my heart, he expects loyalty
Poisoning my love, he expects royalty
Shattering my dreams, he expects my support
My mate is nothing but a shameless moron

In one soundless night, I will lie lonely by his corpse
In one silvery night, I will tear him apart
In my callous bed, I will drag him to hell
In my closed chambers, I will dig his grave.

'O' Men

Summers after summers, winters after winters
I travel across thy gluttonous world
Breaking through walls, sailing through woods
I save thy souls from thy decayed corpse

Death no loss, no mortal understands
Thy fear and run, powerless ye men
Thy new life starts when body become dust
Greet me 'o' humans, here I come

Beautiful my horse, "Whisper" I command
Rides far away proffering tears to all
Enormous my pure cloak mops thy graves
Celestial my crystal dagger cleanses thy spirits again

"God of Death", The Creator calls
His orders I follow: Kill y'all
No pleasure I get to swing my sword
I obey thee, to meet my love…

Mortality is precious, y'all ignorant of
Begging Him for it every dawn, now given up
Years ago, in churchyard, saw her weeping alone
Being immortal, couldn't share her tribulation

God of life, graced me a day
I went to her to see her end
She died in my arms, I held her tight
Failed to trick myself: I "God of Death"

She stays behind the white wall
No path for the Gods to go
Death: the sole path, to meet my love
Death: the only way, to feel her warmth

Restraint of power, thy Gods can't help
Immortality is curse, thy Gods suffer
Tied up with chains, free are y'all
Treasure thy valuable mortality, it's a gift to y'all.

Stay Alive

Each hour witnesses this...
Thousands come; thousands leave
For few we grief, for few we weep
Few engraved thy names so deep

What they had the others didn't
He made alike, same hands and minds
Hard work & dedication can't be all
Passion & Valiance must be there after all

Dream chooses no royalties or prosperous
They blooms in the hearts of all.
Big or small never matters at all
Passion to procure should be the focus overall

Trail to dream never covered with rose
Thorns, hinges paved at each curl
Few brave hearts bleed miles to stride
They have power to seize; They overpower the maze of pleas

Many dreams faded in nights; many desires died with time
Few dreams still breathe, for them I shall live
Each step towards them, makes me smile
Peace strolls around, I still walk meanwhile

Death is the fear like all I suffice
He made alike, same hands and minds
Every moment I choose to recite
Dreams wrapped with zeal stays alive

Footsteps of mine will be sealed on the dunes of time
Thorns and hinges will fail to tie
Breathe without hope, valueless to life
Life without dream, worthless to live

Falling and standing ain't so easy
Ma' friends, berm to dreams are edgy
Walking to grave, trying and trying
Again ma' friends never fail to thrive

As thousands have come and hundreds have left,
For few we grief, for few we weep
Coz few have engraved thy names so deep.

My Daughter

Glorifying me with eternal love, she came into my life
Gracing me with divine emotions, she walked into my life
Embracing me with the joy of fatherhood, she strolled into my life
She is not just my daughter; she is the purpose of my life.

The day I held her for the first time, I knew she would shine all her
life
The day I saw her sparkling eyes, I knew she was going to rise
The day she blossomed my home with her smile, I knew she would
boost the whole mankind
She is not just my daughter; she is the fruit of my life.

Along with the running time, she flowered with kindness and
elegance
The fragrance of her goodness, the saga of her beauty spread across
far miles
When people admired her success, my face glimmered with delight
When people praised her actions, my heart pounded with pride
She is not just my daughter; she is the meaning of my life.

Every day and night of my life echoed with her sacred voice
Every day and night of my life bloomed with her thriving mind
Every day and night of my life revolved around her grace and smile
She is not just my daughter; she is the dream of my life.

But nothing ever then happened according to the thoughts of mine,
My daughter was restless, so was the harsh time
Her innocence was ripped apart, so was her virtues in life
Every wish of her burned into ashes in that ruthless night.

Her body thrived in pain when the evil empowered with disgrace
Her soul was raped when the evil mopped all her goodness
Every inch of her hope was mangled when the ravishing lust molded its way.

Today I see her fighting with life
Today I see her growling in pain
Today I see her cursing her life
Today I see her sobbing every moment

The sparks in her eyes have faded away
The tears of her have washed her hopes away
Now every moment in her life, she wants to run away
But she is not just my daughter; she is the light of my life.

Standing beside her while hiding my own pain
Showing her the path to light, while I have lost my own trail
Assembling her shattered dreams while I am broken into pieces
Teaching her to never give up while I'm clueless have become the motive of my life

For the shining days she had gifted me, I will never let her loose
the battle of life
For the pride that gratified my existence, I will always hold her
tight
As she is not just my daughter, she is more than my life
I will fight with whole world and her to preach her how to survive

She is not just my daughter, she is the hope of my life
She is not just my daughter; she is the fruit of my life.
She is not just my daughter; she is the dream of my life.
And she is not just my daughter; she is the god's grace in disguise.

Koraput

I see the sun rising, I see the moon hiding
I see the petals falling, I see the barks decaying
I see the flowers blossoming; I see the leaves fading
I see the animals waking, I see the birds fluttering
I see all but nobody sees me, I feel all but nobody feels me

Days are passing away, Years are flying away
I am at the same place lost in the maze of time

I see the rain mating with the soil
I see the autumn painting the hills
I see the winter cuddling the drooping leaves
I see the clouds crowning the edge of tall trees
I see all but nobody sees me, I feel all but nobody feels me

While there was that time where all was fine
While there was that time where all were mine
The dazzling moonshine illuminated thy fate
The warm sunrays appraised thy days
The fragranced bud mingled with thy scent

These were the days when all saw me & was fine
These were the days when all felt me & was mine

Coiled in the garland of fate, I see myself hung on the wall
Stumbled by the bumps of dole, I see thy love weeping

Scared by parent's misery, I see them buried in grief
I see my bones strayed in ashes
While I see all, nobody sees me
While I feel all, nobody feels me

In the dark woods of Koraput, I craved for my life
Under the frosty shades of Koraput, I lost my life
While thy body is gone, spirit is still alive
While thy sins have evanesced, virtue is still alive
While I see all, nobody sees me
While I feel all, nobody feels me.

The Other Side

While the mysterious silence wraps the trees
While the daylong tiredness decimates from the body
While the lashes mate delicately in the dark night
My soul detaches from body; flees across thousands of realms
My soul travels across the dark seas; visits the glorious cities

While the world snores in the warmth of the blanket
While the leaves sway the layers of dust
While the tides roar out the pain of the clashes
My soul hovers over the ocean of hopes; feels the peace among all
My soul sees the friendship across the invisible boundaries; feels
only love among all

While the moonlight ornaments the golden deserts
While the folks ponder over their pending pursuits
My soul hears the growl of needy; feels the pain of hunger
My soul sees the wall between death & life; sees the shadows of
miserable spirits

In the visits across the wall of death
I see few spirits mourning; few spirits celebrating
I hear few spirits complaining; few spirits appreciating
I see one white shadow staring, and staring

The pain in her eyes narrates me her sorrowful misery
The tear in her eyes expresses me her agony in past life

While I meet her every night; she shows me glimpses of her past
life
She danced in the fields of maize
She sang in the arms of her love
She cuddled her mom day and night
She was lovely and bright
One day she went to play in the sea
Next her body was drifting on the bed of sea
That was the hasty end of her life
That was the mournful conclusion of her life
No chance to say the loved one's goodbye
No chance to thank the loved ones for their sacrifice

Every night I travel to feel her pain
Every night I travel to ease her pain
Every night I travel to meet her there
Every night I travel to console her there

Every night now my attempts are going in vain
Every night I just spent searching her in her cell
Every night now I fail to heal her twinge of torment

Now she is gone, so as her misery has gone
Now she is gone, so as her story has gone
Every night now I travel across the realms
Every night now I travel to the other side of life.

Difference

Different was I so were they
Different was my culture so were theirs
Different was my sacraments so were theirs
Different were my opinions so were theirs

"Honor of the family lies in your veil
Don't laugh loudly what people will say
Respect older men, don't sit with them
Keeping your eyes down, symbolizes gracefulness"

Whining about the arrangements; Caviling about the services
They welcome the fresh bride
Years of savings; millions of dreams
Become valueless in no time

Bloodline who never cared; become their allies
Pointing the pettiness is all in their minds
Loaded with ridicules, I feel so futile
Educated and Independent, I belong to this time

Ink and pen are my companion tonight
Family was my radical; I am their powerful knight
Draped in red; I condemn such conviction
Ornamented with gold; I fight against such expression

Different am I so are they
Different is my culture so is theirs
Different are my sacraments so are theirs
Different are my opinions so are theirs

Different are nights and days
Different are men and women
Different cannot be the reason for differences
Different cannot glorify impudence

Different are I and my husband
Different are my families and my in-laws
Different are our ethics and cultures
Different cannot justify such narrowness.

Doorway

Several years have glided away
Yet this small place remains the same
The uproar of the sea still hinders the hymn of wind
The chorus of devotees still rattles the cold breeze

Several years have passed away
The mass has grown old so do I
Yet I see the withered man standing at the doorway
Yet I see the same reluctance to step beyond the gateway

Time matured me yet I never lost focus on him
Work engrossed me yet I never lost interest in him
Received ample opportunities yet I never faced him
Overheard hundreds of tales yet never believed in them

Several years have sailed away
Still my courage wanes away
When I stand near to him
All my thoughts fade away

Several years have slipped away
Yet I witness the murkiness in his eyes
Yet I hear the remorse in his prayers
Still I stand clueless about his wish

Again, I stand close by, having the faith that I can ask him
Again, I stand beside him, having the faith that he will answer me
Again, I feel the enigmatic silence tantalizing me
Again, I feel the gush of impatience trembling the confidence in me

Dragging me through the crowd, he shook me from inside
Shivering in grief, he patiently asked me to reside
He confessed about his piercing misery that eve
He divulged that he comes to seek death every eve
He revealed that he once drenched in vengeance
He stated that he once squandered in violence
He proclaimed that his one country was torn into two
He declared that the religion once he followed is now untrue

He swamped in the blood of his own one noon
He strangled his only love in that full moon
Romance and affection, he buried that night
Viciously choked his only love until she died

Several years have passed away
Inch of pain has not grayed away
The revenge that possessed him
With time it has killed him

Several years have hovered away
Yet he stands at the temple gateway
Several years have flown away
Yet I stand with him at the same doorway.

Dream… the Misery, the Joy

Never has been easy to determine the depth of my dreams
Sometimes they look so real and sometimes so dim
Sometimes they astound me, sometimes they petrify me
Sometimes they soothe me, sometimes they oppress me

Like veiled trails, dreams are full of delight and hindrance
Like the uncanny sea, dreams are full of noise and silence
Sometimes they fathom me, sometimes they humiliate me
Sometimes they embrace me, sometimes they smother me

Yet among all dreams, one dream I reminisce
Yet among all dreams, one dream still terrorizes
The screams, the fear, those nights of tremor
The pain, the agony, those nights became darker

Ruthless was the soul that haunted me nights after nights
Merciless was the soul that defiled me nights after nights
Tearing me apart, ripping me apart was his pass of time
Death was tender than the torment in those sleepless nights

The twitch of pain that I suffered, I wanted to express around
The assault that I resisted every night, I wished to say it aloud
Being the victim, being the captive was the story of my nights
Being sabotaged, being shamed was the reality of my nights

Now the time has passed away, now the years have fled away
Endless attempts have shut the pricking pain away
The visions of the dreams have gradually faded away
The screams in my dreams have calmed away

Yet I reflect the same thoughts again and again
Yet I utter the same words again and again
Never has been easy to determine the depth of the dream
Sometimes they look so real and sometimes so dim.

It

The failure of morals in self gives birth to it
The possession of the soul by ego further nurtures it

They say it decays your crux and makes you empty
They say it taints your future and makes you wobbly

Yet here I stand, pondering about every trick of it
Yet here I stand, addressing every torment of it

The storm it creates in me bounds me to hate myself
The resent it breeds in me inflicts me to end myself

Yet here I stand again loving myself
Yet here I stand again forgiving myself

The darkness in it transcends the sinful prison in the hell
The agony in it surpasses the misery in the cell

The perseverance in it to disrobe me, startles me
The passion in it to toxify me, astounds me

I sense it is clogging me, I feel it is languishing me
Yet here I stand again persuading myself
Yet here I stand again enlivening myself

And here I stand again facing my guilt
And here I stand again speaking to my guilt

The avidity in you cherishes the goodness in me
The firmness in you bolsters the remaining faith in me

The saga of your victories inspires me to defeat you
The cold mocking of yours enforces me to combat you

And here I will always stand to crush you
And here I will always stand to learn from you
And here I will always stand to conquer you.

I

I woke up in the middle of a frosty night
Quivering and trembling with an uncanny fear
I, facing myself in the dream was strikingly unclear
Standing amidst the shadow of jitters
He digs my past …
He reveals about me "Who was I?" and "What was I" in my previous birth

He said I was once at peace, He said I was once at harmony
He said I owned the magical aura, He said I enshrined with eternal love
He said I was a kind man that transformed several lives
He said I was an honorable man that gleamed many eyes

I dismay myself as this can't be the real me
I hide myself as they shouldn't see this new me

He protests I tainted his purity
He whines I soiled his sanity
And I say…This ain't me: this can't be me

I kill people; I bath with their blood
I traumatize people; I relish their pain
I am a savage, I am a murderer
I am a devil & "God of Vengeance"

He disagrees-I am the evil
He believes- I can be cured
He says I was known as The Socrates
My words smudge the history about me
I am the Destroyer: I am the Killer
I am a Sadist: I am called now as The Hitler

Never shall the world know about the saint in me
Never shall the world hear about the angel in me
Thou tried to mold the goodness in me
Yet I choose the unholy in me
I am wicked; I hate the world around me
So, when I die; I will doom the world with me.

You in Me

The hands with which you hold me
The eyes with which you look at me
The smile of yours mesmerizes me
You empower me, you strengthen me
I want to be with you, and you are forever in me

In the darkness of my life, you hold me tight
You magnify the love in me, you amplify the passion in me
You relinquish me of my pain, you discharge me from my burden
You are the nature, you are the Creator
You are the world, you are the star
You are the fire, you are the destroyer
You are mine and I am yours

The shadow of yours show me the way
The image of yours defines me everywhere
I sing the sagas of our meetings in my dreams
I obey the words you murmur to me
They laugh at me, saying me insane
They mock at me, saying me fool
Yet I wake up every morning in amaze
Today I declare "I love you My Grace"

The mass say I fake to entertain
The people say I crave to seek acclaim

Now onwards I really do not care
No onwards I am indifferent
All are yours and you are mine
I recite this all the time

You the epitome of chastity, you the icon of serenity
You the crux of knowledge, you the source of wisdom
You are the beauty, you are the beast
"My Lord, My Grace, I know you are behind all of this"

Nobody can treasure the emotions in me
Nobody can acknowledge the pleasure in me
All fail to understand the joy of being with you
All fail to accept that one can genuinely love you

You the father, You the Creator
You the mentor, you the destroyer
Loving you is all I am capable of
Loving you is all I could learn from the all
Loving you made be love your world
Loving you made me learn the worth of all

Now my life is destined for your love
Till the last breath I will love you and all of yours
Until I reach my grave, I will worship you and all of yours.

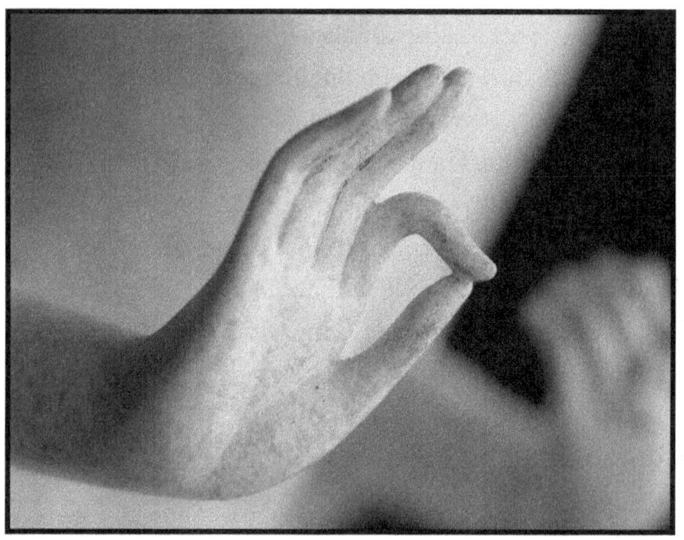

Pursue

Uplifts the curtains, Hails the sun
As the night withers, HE applauds your passion
Ennobles the frosty dews; adulates the cherry blossoms
Embodies wisdom, HE is God's incarnation

Crystals from peaks; flow to seek
Cleanses thy frail body, molds taupe to pink
No dirt no taint they rinse, sways chastity and peace
Melding with the holy rill; every drop bestows reprieve

Swarms of footsteps squire to pursue
Bleeding red they rumble your virtues
Pain and Agony nothing they feel
Your love so cogent; strives to heal

Power and Moksha; thy deeply accomplished
Seven weeks devoted without any feed
Noblest of all; endorses the old oak tree
Enlightenment of Him; Death of my Prince…

Merrier than ever; jubilant than ever
Mellowed together besides the plum dale
Love and passion fostered since ever
Oblivious of it; he raced away forever

Golden his skin; I felt from within
Cold and warm; I fondled in my dream
Beautiful his eyes; glittered in grin
Day and night, I slumped in swain

Flames of love; eluding my visions
Roar of urge; impairing my reflections
No pain no sorrow no other sensation
My heart swooped in his passion

Purple was the sky, color of adoration
Striding across the ferns; I marched towards my destination
Love shall be expressed without any vacillation
Redder grew the roses, embracing my affection

Vicious wind blew athwart the north
Few miles were left; trail turned forlorn
Murky was the sky, no trace of sun
Purple was gone; grey was upsurge

Jittery was my heart; I dreamt so long
Life and death were far no more
Anxious footsteps were clogged by fear
Amidst the bush, a known shadow appears

Beautiful his eyes; full of grim
No love no mercy they enshrine
"Cycle of rebirth, I need to explore
No family no friends; I tend to endeavor"

Last were his words, quiver in my ears
Drenched in anguish; I imbibed my tears
Love is giving; I bid him farewell
Oblivious of it; He waned in thin air

Epitome of Peace; he pledges *Nirvana*
Rebirth of God; he attained *samsara*
Father of the World; he abetted all
Creator of the Nature; he charted all

Love was all; I opined for
No wisdom or sanity; I had craved for
In quest of prudence, he marooned all
In flare of loss, my life is dour

Flames of love; distorts my visions
Roar of urge; blurs my reflections
Only pain and sorrow are my companions
Death is thy serf; give me your salvation.

Last Winter

Hoary clouds frowned day and night
Frosty balls spilled over hillsides
Shrouded the fawn glebe in daylight
White as pearl the terrain shines

Snowy bed snuggles up tight
Cradles the fury canines in twilight
Warmth and blaze their hearts pine
Delusive winter fails to suffice

Church bell far across the riverside
Jangles in pain, bawls all night
Ivory winds from top hills
Sway through lanes, whistle to deride

Fall in December, the cruelest emperor
Envenoms the crops, propels peasants to sadness
Fall in December, the vicious juncture
Lynched my life, clogged my future

Dawn till dusk, He brewed in lust
Scared our fates and Lily's trust
Sordid hands ripped Lily's soul
Once asserted to protect her

Widowed early; lost my mate
Wealthy Caesar emphasized to aid
Cleaning mansion not beneath my honor
Dolls and moppets danced at all corners

Little Lily, my brightest flower
Cloaked with grace; crowned with benevolence
Little Lilly, my fairytale
Overwhelmed with puppets, lived like a princess

All kindness, no demands
Caesar played with her in high regards
Three sons so brave, no daughters but he craves
Again, and again he pledged, "Lily my light, I will save"

Summers and monsoons all passed
Lily my blossom crouched in doom
No songs no dance, nothing coaxed
Lily my blossom quivered in distress

December the month, chilly was the noon
Cleaned the hall, rushed to Lord's room
Sunk in tears, Lily choked with fear
Stood naked, no trace of attire

Lecherous Caesar, drowned in wine
Lunched his tongue, sucked her divine
Filthy hands all over her body
Shredding her innocence: will survive

Fair her body injured to blue
Wounds of rape dried to puce
Loins of reckless body continues to bloom
Staring at me he dares to ridicule

December the month, chilly was the noon
Far across the riverside, church bell roars in gloom
No courage, no money, only motherhood
Justice had to be done in that gaudy room

Mightiest the knife, snagged to strike
Stabbed the ravisher, until he dies
Swamp of blood flooded his fancy hive
My hands strived to strike, and strike

Outside the castle, harsh winter was on its ride
Hoary clouds frowned in daylight
Frosty balls spilled over naive hillsides
Shrouded the mushy glebe in pride

Fall in December: the cruelest Emperor
Envenoms the innocence, propels to distress
Fall in December: the vicious juncture
Lynched my life, made me the Killer.

With Her

Thoughts about her were running in my mind.
The light of evolution was burning all night.
The secrets about her weakness were getting revealed.
She was full of worries and miseries, yet her face blazed with glee

She challenged me yet nourished me.
She grumbled at me yet admired me.
Her thoughts were clean and serene, while her words were harsh and mean.
Every time she looked at me, her eyes sparkled with gleam.
Every time she preached me, her words were wrapped with concern and hope.
Every time she appreciated me, her face blushed with pride.

Being the shield, being the steel wasn't very easy
She denied of many things, she ignored my feelings,
yet she holds me in my grieving
She claims she shall never expect yet she craves for my success

She declares she shall never wish yet she adores my grace .
Every moment I had spent with her, was a pleasure to me.
Every words she spoke was fruitful to me.
Every expression of her, delighted me
Whenever I ponder, I realize she was a teacher to me

The Final Verdict
Verse 1

Colossal hall echoed with mystical calmness
Luculent floor sparkled with eternal eagerness
Gigantic walls bowed in great honor
Frisky stars twinkled at every corner

Vitreous chambers dazzled with wisdom
Ivory ceiling glittered with diamonds
Silver lilies embellished the chandeliers
Imperial founts magnified the grandeur

Away from the mighty sun
Deep beneath the ocean
Before the era of human's inception
Almighty devised His holy mansion

Overwhelmed with His divine glory
This moment narrates His felicitous theory
Today's Chronicle; His ultimate prophecy
Today's world, tomorrow's History

Verse 2

Debarking from diverse dominions, Lords descend at the Pylon
Before the break of dawn, thy sail towards the destination
Soon shall they march in the mansion!
Soon shall they announce the final conclusion!

Ethereal as feather, flits the saddle
Balletic like autumn, the swans ride the chariot
Gliding the effulgent veil, infusing the beguiling scent
Arrives, Lordess Aerial, the epitome of freedom

Through the cliffs, arrives an azure wagon
Adorned with stars, Orion, Lyra other constellations
Scepter in a hand, Lord Sky guides every clime
Prism in the other, reflects the seven rays of light

Knight of the castle, ruler of the waves' motions
Seated on doughty sea horse, enters the Lord Ocean
No ornaments or gears are part of thy possession
Master of patience, he calms world's agitation

Flames of wisdom ignited far across the coral wings
Drifting through the radiant sun, arrives the noble phoenix
Valiant sword as long as the Nile, dangled across His brawny waist
Lord Fire, Master of Heat, patiently cleanses all the waste

Carved with fine design, arrives Sandalwood caisson
Unicorns, Lions and tuskers, the prominent animation
Timber colored chariot carpeted with mauve velour
Strides out, Lord Earth; the patriarch of Universe

Verse 3

Pacing through the gallery, the five lords march in elegance
Unbolting the limpid door, the Jury assembles in the hall of justness
Today the final sentence shall be guarded from prejudice!!
Today shall be the final verdict: Man, Guilty or Not Guilty

Prosecutor Methuselah: the first creation of God
Commander of Mother Nature, the mentor of earth
Grieved with time, Immortal Methuselah cited malicious crimes
Donned in black rob, she vows to avenge the martyrs of strife

Defense council" Samay": The messenger of God
Subtle and tolerant, witnessed the journey of Earth
Odyssey: Evolution of life till bloodshed in Armageddon
Quietly archived thy activities of life, Samay the last hope of the mankind

Above All, stands the creator of all
Cloaked in white, he greets all
Blissful he seems, as if he fathomed the ending
Accosted all, "Let's start with the proceedings"

Verse 4

"Lauded every dawn, wailed every night, centuries through I lit the beacon
Applauded inventions, sobbed for failures, years through I aspired their elation
Yet one day, they abhorred me, huddled with an axe
Yet one day, they slaughtered the innocents, seared all into ash
Atrocious Murderers, barbarous the mankind
Methuselah, your trustful curator demands heads of all alive
Death, the sole penance, shall serve them right"

"Methuselah, the holy tree, primed of all
I bow with gratitude, shall counter few charges not all
Humans not scavengers, they are curious after all
Limitless are their thoughts with no boundaries and walls
Gods' eminent creation, woman the kindest of all
Messenger of God, I have witnessed their fall; Cruel are few, rest are harmless souls
Death, the sole penance, shall not suit all"

"Complexity their kernel, my coveted belief
Every felony they committed, I choose to reprieve
Blinded by their endeavor, I ignored their greed
Oblivious of their frontier, I oppressed my instincts
Ages have past, their hunger surpassed

Killed millions they still disregard
The oldest tree, I, was once in their trap, pleaded for justice: Man
shall never regard"

"Millions kill, thousands save
Millions provoke, thousands conserve
Millions are greedy, thousands serve needy
Millions burn in lust, thousands sacrifice in love
Millions oppress in pride, thousands struggle to revive
Millions dogged in jealousy, thousands aid ardently
I, the reflection of time, shall testify for Millions' crime yet fight for
thousands of lives"

"Blame the only game, man mastered all life
Cursed the God, the Nature for self-vice
Gloomed in gluttony, fostered desires
The woods, the wilds fizzled to respire
The cliffs, the streams, once content with bliss
Now tainted with smog, infected with cig
Man, aptly dipped paradise into pit, Man are the convicts, and I
shall not retreat"

"Oh, mighty Methuselah, I deny truce, I refuse forgiveness
I clamor for justice, I ask for probity
For rebuild of paradise, I see our last opportunity

Though heads of all, shall not resolve all
Humans shall then be equal to us
Killing innocents, the crime they trialed for
Same allegations shall be then bestowed on us
Justice should be free from prejudice and anger
Men are demons, we are their mentors"

"Hints and chances, Men had enough of it
Nature hits back, we pronounced it
Floods, Hurricanes other calamities warned them about their limits
Imprudent men chose death in war and epidemics
War and disease thy the proud inventors of it
Killed for land, women, money and fake conceit
Innocents are none, all possess slightest deceit
Self above the world, their only creed"

"Years ago, a mistake was done
Mistake was not the birth of humans
The fault was in Almighty's creation
Ego, anger, love, greed these are complex emotions
For mastering them we spent years in meditation
Now the chance for few to follow the right direction
Beheading all now is that mistake's repetition"

Verse 5

"Hours already consumed in cogent deliberation
Both evenly utilized their chances of articulation
Now shall I give the fair chance of summation!!
The last opportunity to express thy final reflection
Then shall the Lord, The Jury shall pronounce the final decision"

"Samay, my beloved friend I concur, Love is a complex emotion
Love deepens passion, love muddles wisdom
Yet Love, the uncharted notion was not God's creation
He regarded, Love, the source of elation, deserves celebration
He formed humans, his children with love and dedication
He claimed humans were messenger of his love and devotion
Love urges balance, love endorses control, and love preaches compassion
Since years love compelled us to neglect their thrill to destruction
Turned the world into slaughterhouse, they still say love is the reason
All my mighty lords, I remember that era, the world before devastation
Lord Aerial danced with the mauve winds applauded the old mates' reunion
Lord Earth aroused the lilies while couples swore to love each other till perpetuation
Lord Fire scorched the desire of love, warmed bodies in frozen nights across the horizon
Lord Sky illuminated the sky with seven colors, when father returned to son for vacation

Love Aqua cushioned the unborn in mother's womb, protects the divine love from pollution
I, the old tree, sang with the cuckoos to wither the pain of heartbreak and affliction
Samay, you the biggest healer, opened their doors to hope and consolation
Love the forceful entity, we all summon
Love the divine prophecy, we all listen
Love of humans, is not the only love
Love of trees, animals, flowers possess the same affection
Worshipping one kinds' love, letting others' die, an intolerable action
Humans buried God's sole ambition; Humans burnt God's glorious intention
God and my dear Lords, I am incapable of any further absolution
Guilty are humans, Death shall only serve their treason"

"Powerful all words, I worship you my friend
Being a mother, you still condemn
I ain't the lady, still hope for their chance
You the epitome of kindness, yet end of them is your demand
Millions of their terrible crimes, I shall fail to strike
Nasties are they; I shall never decline
God's greatest obsession was human
In glistening nights, I heard God's adoration
In thundering nights, I observed God's contrition

Here am I fighting to protect his intention
Here am I fighting to save his exertion

All are not evil, few bear his soul
Hope is a beautiful thing, please do not kill all
God is the person who is hurtful the most
Agony in his heart is echoing across the hall
I kneel today and pray for forgiveness
Save few to recreate the beautiful world
Love may not be his creation but his inspiration after all
Whatever now shall be, I ought to obey lords' final verdict in this hall

Verse 6

"Samay and Methuselah, Thank you my children
Both served the purpose, both fought well
Human vs Nature, never the intended war
Human part of Nature, was faith behind all
One family, one father, one home, the earth
Yet one child rose to power, abandoned the rest
My blood, your blood, their blood the same
Nature, the benevolent sister, generously only gave
Yet human, the cunning brother, thanklessly craved
Beyond justice there is nothing shall I evangelize
Nimble were the humans, they were my pride
Kind was the nature, they dignified my presence
I mourned in solitude while my children squabbled
My heart shivered in anguish while my blood shed in vain
I am the father, all my children are same
I am the father and I shall not claim
I choose the Jury to decide on this final day
Before the final verdict that mighty Lords' declare
I repeat; Love is same for all and shall remain
Men and Nature are my children and shall remain
Balance, the sole key to sustain, I had trained
Justice shall be shielded for prejudice, I proclaim
The punishment of the trial, Lords must intuit
If men committed sin, then shall be chastened
Jury shall now vote Men Guilty or Not Guilty
Jury shall now give the final verdict Men Guilty or Not Guilty
Jury shall now soon end this Final Summit"

About the Author

Satabdi Mohanty

Date of birth : 04th June, 1991

Place of birth : Bhubaneswar

Email | satabdi4.mohanty@gmail.com

Instagram | https://www.instagram.com/satabdiexpresses

Satabdi Mohanty works as a consultant in an IT multinational company. She holds MBA degree from Great Lakes Institute of Management, Chennai. She started writing at a young age and gradually it became her form of meditation. Her biggest strength is that she is a compassionate individual who feels the varied emotions around her. Her favourite poet is Robert Browning. After years of writing for herself, she has finally decided to bring out her first book, a collection of her poems which emphasizes on varied human emotions and injustice towards the nature.

Special Thanks

(names listed alphabetically)

Aayushi Bhardwaj	Mridula Malav
Abhishek Parija	Nitish C
Adarsh Anurag	Parul Batra
Ajay Kumar	Pragati Sah
Akash Ranjan	Pranitha B
Akhilesh Singh	Pratip Bhattacharyya
Asim Mohanty	Pulkit Goyal
Avinash Kumar	Rajeev Nanda
Bibek Mohanty	Rakesh Kamath G
Bibhudutta Mohanty	Reetika Bhattacharjee
Biswadeep Mohanty	Satpql Kaur
Charu Naimisha	Shakti Mohanty
Devanshu Arya	Shashank Kumar
Devashish Saun	Shipra Marik
Ebin Mathew	Shivam Sinha
Gurdeep Kaur	Shraddha Mitra
Hardik Thakker	Sourabha SN
Ishan Shekhar	Sudipto Ghosh
Jazon Khan	Sulagna Mohanty
Karthik Malli	Suman Ranjita Singh
Lakshay Handa	Surbhit Arora
Megha Singh	Toshi Sharma
Mithilesh Kumar	Vivek Singh

An Elusive Repose

SATABDI MOHANTY

Email your questions, experiences,
and suggestions to the author at
satabdi4.mohanty@gmail.com

Your Experiences